Read & Respond

FOR
KS1

Read & Respond

FOR KS1

Authors: Elaine Hampton and Karen Leigh

Editor: Victoria Lee

Assistant Editor: Rachel Mackinnon

Series Designer: Anna Oliwa

Designer: Erik Ivens

Illustrations: Helen Oxenbury

Text © 2006 Elaine Hampton and Karen Leigh
© 2006 Scholastic Ltd

Designed using Adobe InDesign

Published by Scholastic Ltd, Villiers House,
Clarendon Avenue, Leamington Spa,
Warwickshire CV32 5PR

www.scholastic.co.uk

Printed by Bell & Bain
2 3 4 5 6 7 8 9   7 8 9 0 1 2 3 4 5

British Library Cataloguing-in-Publication Data
A catalogue record for this book is available from the British
Library.
ISBN 0-439-94491-0   ISBN 978-0439-94491-5

Acknowledgements

The publishers gratefully acknowledge permission to reproduce
the following copyright material: **Walker Books Ltd** for the use of
the front cover of the book, text and illustrations from *We're Going
on a Bear Hunt* by Michael Rosen. Text © 1989, Michael Rosen,
Illustrations © 1989, Helen Oxenbury (1989, Walker Books Ltd).
Every effort has been made to trace copyright holders for the works
reproduced in this book, and the publishers apologise for any
inadvertent omissions.

We're Going on a Bear Hunt

About the book

We're Going on a Bear Hunt follows a family as they travel through the deep grass of a field, across a river, through some oozy mud, journey through a dark forest, experience a snowstorm and finally find what they have been searching for in a dark cave.

However having found the bear they realise they are not quite as brave as they thought they were and rapidly retrace their steps with the bear chasing them all the way home. It's a fantastic journey but was it real or imagined?

We're Going on a Bear Hunt offers a clear, repetitive text, which makes it ideal for readers to revisit frequently, building their confidence to read independently. The text is excellent for reading aloud and offers many opportunities for children's active participation.

The book would also be an ideal choice when planning reading and writing activities linked to the theme of familiar settings and when selecting stories and rhymes with predictable and repeating patterns. It is ideal for linking in with Year 1 and Year 2 objectives from the National Literacy Strategy.

Finally, Helen Oxenbury's detailed illustrations, a mix of colour and black and white, are full of life and action and provide plenty of scope for discussion about the family's activities with opportunities for oral storytelling beyond the text. The plight of the poor, lonely bear is poignantly highlighted in the final illustration as he trudges back to his cave.

About the author

Michael Rosen was born in the London suburb of Pinner in 1946. Both of his parents were teachers.

On leaving school he first started training as a doctor at the Middlesex Hospital Medical School, but then eventually switched to study English at Wadham College, Oxford.

Most of his time at university was spent doing theatre work – writing, acting and directing. He finally became a writer and his first collection of poems for children called 'Mind Your Own Business' was published in 1974.

Since then Michael has written and edited many anthologies of poems and has, of course, written many children's picture books including *We're Going on a Bear Hunt* which was first published in 1989 by Walker Books Ltd.

Michael writes 'stuff' and doesn't mind whether it's called poetry or not, but he likes writing that sort of thing and children like reading it.

Most of his adult life has been spent as a freelance writer, journalist, performer and broadcaster. Michael says he usually calls himself a writer and broadcaster though some people call him a poet and performer – he spends a lot of time in schools conducting his 'one man show'.

> **Facts and figures**
> *We're Going On a Bear Hunt*
> First published in 1989 by Walker Books.
> It has won five awards including the 1990 Smarties Children's Book of the Year Award.
> **Michael Rosen**
> He has won other awards including the International Reading Association Teachers Choice Award in 1999 (US) for his Classic Poetry Collection and the National Literacy WOW Award in 2005 for his 'Alphabet Poem'.

Guided reading

The cover

Look together at the cover of *We're Going on a Bear Hunt*. Ask the children to point to the title of the book and to read it. Let them point to the two names underneath the title. Discuss the different roles of the author and illustrator.

Ask the children to describe the people on the front of the book and what they are doing. (A family going on a walk.) Encourage the children to use the word 'characters'. Do they think these characters will appear in the story? Where do they think the family is going? Refer to the title of the book: what is a 'bear hunt'? Do people really go on bear hunts? Would any of the children like to go on a bear hunt? Where would they go on one?

Look at the back cover and discuss the girl and the dog. Who are they? Open the book out flat to show that they are part of the family on the front cover. Using the title and picture clues, ask the children to offer suggestions of other characters that might be in the story.

First reading

The first time you read the story allow the children to enjoy it and become familiar with the repetitive phrases and story as a whole. On subsequent readings focus on particular areas, as discussed in the sections below.

Going to catch a big one!

Start reading the story with the children, encouraging them to join in. Read up to the point where they go through the grass '…Swishy swashy!'. Look at the black and white illustration, on the previous page. Ask the children to describe what is happening in the picture. (The baby is having a piggyback ride; the little boy has a stick.) Can they suggest any actions for the text: 'We can't go over it. We can't go under it. Oh no! We've got to go through it!'?

Turn to the next page. Ask the children to comment on the difference between this page and the previous one. (This one is in colour.)

Read together the words: 'Swishy swashy'. What do these words describe? (The sound of the grass.) Can the children offer suggestions for other words that could be used to describe this noise?

Ask the children to point to the letter that has changed in the word 'swishy' to make the word 'swashy'. What do they notice about the size of the writing? Why is the font size increasing? (As the characters run faster the noise gets louder.)

Ask the children to describe other features in the illustration. Draw their attention to the birds in the sky. What is the correct name for a lot of birds together? What do the children think disturbed the flock of birds?

River, mud and trees

Look together at the illustration on the double-page spread which shows the family standing next to a river. Ask the children where the characters are now. What are they looking at? Read the text, drawing attention to the use of full stops and exclamation marks.

Turn over the page and read together. What do the words describe on this page? Encourage the children to raise their voices as the text gets bigger.

Look carefully at the illustration: what are the family holding in their hands? (Shoes.) Why do they think the characters are doing this? Why has the baby still got her shoes on? Discuss the dangers of crossing a river. Can the children offer suggestions as to what the baby might be saying?

Read on to '…We've got to go through it.' What is happening in the illustration? (The boy is throwing mud or stones while he is waiting for the others, for example.) What might Dad be thinking?

Read the next page. What has happened to the shoes again? Who is carrying them this time! Have the children ever walked through thick mud? Ask them to suggest other words that could be used to describe the sound of feet going through mud.

Continue reading as the family reach the

forest. Discuss with the children times when they have been in a forest. What other word is sometimes used? (Wood.) Look at the black and white illustration. What seems to be bothering the girl sitting on the rock? Ask the children for suggestions as to what the other girl is pointing at and why the boy with the stick seems so excited. Does Dad look happy, excited or worried?

Turn the page and read together the words beginning 'Stumble trip!'. Ask the children to explain the meaning of the word 'stumble'. Invite them to think of different words that could be used here.

Look closely at the illustration. Does the forest look a friendly place? Why do the children think the characters are running through it rather than walking?

It's a beautiful day!

Begin reading the double-page spread that describes the snowstorm. Draw the children's attention to the third line of the rhyme: 'What a beautiful day!'. Look at the illustration – does it look like a beautiful day? Ask the children to describe the type of weather they would consider appropriate for a beautiful day. (Clear, blue skies and warm sunshine, perhaps.) Why does it not seem like a beautiful day? Ask the children to point to the words that tell them what the weather is like in the illustration: 'A snowstorm!'. Invite the children to talk about their own experiences of snow.

Ask the children to identify the words in the text that describe the snowstorm: 'swirling whirling'. What is swirling and whirling the snow about? (The wind.) Can the children offer any other suggestions for words that might be used to describe the storm? Point to the use of -ing at the end of the words. Ask the children to think of other words that could be used ending in the same letters.

Turn the page and allow the children time to discuss the illustration before asking them to read the text. What do the words 'Hoooo woooo!' refer to? (The sound of the wind.) Invite the children to make some other sounds that

could be used to describe the wind. How would they spell them? Have they ever seen words with that many o's in them before? What effect do they think Michael Rosen was trying to create?

The bear

Look together at the illustration of the family standing at the entrance to the cave. Ask children to offer suggestions as to what the characters might be thinking. Why do they think the baby is pulling on the little girl's dress? What do they think is wrong with the dog? (He can sense the bear, or is afraid of the cave.)

Discuss with the children their experiences of caves and what they look like, where they are found and what they smell like. Read together the text. Do the children think the family are scared of going into the cave?

Turn over and read together the next double-page spread. Why do the children think that the characters tiptoe into the cave? Ask the children to point to the words 'WHAT'S THAT?'. What do they notice about these two words? (They are written in capital letters.) Ask the children to offer their own explanations as to why this is so.

Turn to the next page and give the children time to explore the illustration. Read together the text. Draw their attention to the use of four exclamation marks after the word 'BEAR'. Why do they think the author has used so many? Ask the children to explain why yet again the final line of writing on this page is in capital letters. Ask them if they were reading this book aloud how they think this last line should be read. (Shouted.)

Ask the children to look closely at the illustration of the bear. Does he look fierce? Who do they think is more scared – the bear or the dog? Where have the rest of the characters gone?

The chase

Read together the two pages that describe the family's race back through the cave, snowstorm and so on. Ask the children to look closely at

Guided reading

the long narrow illustrations and to identify the bear in each one. Why do they think the bear is chasing the family? Ask the children to comment on the way Helen Oxenbury (the illustrator) has decided to illustrate what is happening on these pages. Why do they think she chose to draw long narrow illustrations? How do they alter the reading of the text? (They create an impression of how quickly the family ran back home.)

Turn to the page beginning 'Get to our front door'. Read the double-page spread aloud to the children, using a faster pace. Ask the children to offer suggestions as to why you read it so quickly. (To emphasise how the family are hurrying.)

Read together the last page. Ask the children what they notice about the size of the text. How would this influence the way they read it? Do they think the family really went on a bear hunt or had it been an imaginary journey?

Turn to the end pages. Ask the children to comment on how they think the bear feels. Why do they think he chased the family home? Perhaps he is just lonely and wants to be their friend?

Shared reading

Extract 1

● Read the extract on photocopiable page 8.
● Read the extract again up to '…We're not scared.'
● Discuss with the children who could be going on a bear hunt. Are they really hunting for bears? Where do they think someone should go if they wanted to catch a bear?
● Look at the picture. Do the people in the picture look like the sort of people you would imagine going on a bear hunt?
● Highlight the word 'beautiful'. Talk about the use of the word. Ask the children what they think would be a beautiful day. List alternative words.
● Look together at the line 'We're not scared'. Discuss why the characters say this – people would usually be scared if they were hunting for bears. Are they trying to be brave?
● Read the rest of the extract. Ask the children to identify the problem the characters have – long wavy grass. Why are they not able to go over or under it? How would they walk through it? List other ways to describe the grass and how it might feel.

Extract 2

● Read extract 2 on photocopiable page 9.
● Re-read the first part of extract 2. Up to 'We can't go under it'. Use plenty of expression and draw the children's attention to the use of exclamation marks.
● Discuss the problem the family are now facing. (A forest.) Let the children point to the words that describe the forest. ('Big' and 'dark'.) Ask for suggestions as to what could be in the forest. What might the dangers be?
● Notice the use of repetition in the text. Can the children offer reasons as to why the author chose to use repetition? Is it effective?
● Read to the end of the extract. Encourage the children to read the lines with you, saying the words louder each time. You may find it useful to use a pointer. Why do they think the text is shown (increasing in size) like this?
● Ask what is causing the characters to 'Stumble trip!' (Roots, for example.) Are there any other words that could be used to describe how they move as they travel through the forest? (For example: Snap crack, as twigs break under their feet.)

Extract 3

● Read, as a whole class, an enlarged copy of the text on photocopiable page 10. Use a pointer to encourage one-to-one correspondence with the words in the text and the words read aloud.
● Encourage the children to read using pace and expression by modelling this process as you read. Encourage the children to read quite fast. Ask them how reading quickly portrays what is going on in the story – that the characters are in a hurry, going up and down the stairs. Discuss why you think they forgot to shut the front door. Do you think they would have forgotten to shut the front door if they had not been rushing?
● Ask the children what they notice about the sentences. (They are short.) Why do they think this is? (To emphasise the fact that they are hurrying to get into the house.) Does it help to tell the reader how to read the text?
● Circle the words that are verbs and ask the children what these words do. (They tell us what the characters are doing.) Can the children recall any other similar words in the story? Make a list of any the children remember.
● Ask the children to retell what happens in this extract in their own words, using complete sentences with verbs.

Extract 1

We're going on a bear hunt.
We're going to catch a big one.
What a beautiful day!
We're not scared.

Uh-uh! Grass!
Long wavy grass.
We can't go over it.
We can't go under it.

Oh no!
We've got to go through it!

Text © Michael Rosen; illustration © Helen Oxenbury

Extract 2

Uh-uh! A forest!
A big dark forest.
We can't go over it.
We can't go under it.

Oh no!
We've got to go through it!

Stumble trip!
Stumble trip!
Stumble trip!

Text © Michael Rosen; illustration © Helen Oxenbury

Extract 3

Get to our front door.

Open the door.

Up the stairs.

Oh no!

We forgot to shut the door.

Back downstairs.

Shut the door.

Back upstairs.

Into the bedroom.

Into bed.

Under the covers.

Text © Michael Rosen; illustration © Helen Oxenbury

www.scholastic.co.uk

READ & RESPOND: Activities based on *We're Going on a Bear Hunt*

Plot, character and setting

What now?

> **Objective:** To use simple poetry structures and to substitute own ideas, write new lines.
> **What you need:** Photocopiable page 15, writing materials, flipchart, individual whiteboards and pens.
> **Cross-curricular links:** Geography, Unit 24, Passport to the world.

What to do
● Ask the children to identify all the places the family went through on their adventure. Record them on the flipchart in the correct order.
● Invite the children to write on their whiteboards one other place the family *could* have gone through (for example, the jungle or desert). Encourage them to share their ideas with the class.
● Write down their suggestions. Choose one and encourage the children to think how it would fit into the rhyme.

● Explain that they are going to need to think of two words to describe their new place. Ask for ideas (for example: *jungle* – hot and leafy).
● Together recite the rhyme putting in the new words. Try a few alternatives until you are all satisfied with the choice.
● Hand out the photocopiable sheet. Ask the children to draw and label two alternative places the family could have gone through and then write a new verse based on one of their illustrations.
● Ask some children to share their verses.

> **Differentiation**
> **For older/more able children:** Suggest the children make a list of words that could be used to describe their other illustrations.
> **For younger/less able children:** Let the children choose one other place and, with an adult scribing, offer two descriptive words, which they then copy onto their sheet.

It's a bear!

> **Objective:** To describe characters, expressing own views and using words from texts.
> **What you need:** Photocopiable page 16, writing materials, flipchart, individual whiteboards and pens, copies of *We're Going on a Bear Hunt*, prepared word cards.
> **Cross-curricular links:** Science, Unit 2C, Variation.

What to do
● Ask the children to look together at the illustration of the bear in the cave. Read the text together.
● Ask the children if they have ever seen a bear. Where do bears usually live?
● Can they offer suggestions as to why this bear might live in a cave? Where do they think this cave is? Point out the picture on the end pages which show the bear walking along the beach by the sea. Do bears usually live in caves at the

beach? Where would you expect a bear to live?
● Ask the children to describe the bear in the cave. What colour is he? Is he big or small? List some of their answers on the flipchart.
● Invite the children to suggest how the bear might feel when he encounters the family (for example, frightened or angry).
● Hand out the photocopiable sheet and ask the children to write down individual words and then short sentences to describe the bear.
● Share some of the children's words and sentences. Use some words to make new sentences as a class.

> **Differentiation**
> **For older/more able children:** Challenge the children to carry out some independent research on bears.
> **For younger/less able children:** Show a selection of prepared word cards for the children to choose from to describe the bear.

Plot, character and setting

The river

Objective: To discuss meanings of words and phrases, and sound effects in poetry.
What you need: Photocopiable page 17, writing materials, flipchart, pictures of rivers, individual whiteboards and pens, prepared words on card, copies of *We're Going on a Bear Hunt*.

What to do

● Ask the children to name the different places the family visited. Tell them you are going to discuss the river today. Ask the children if they know what a river is. Is it the same as the sea?
● Show the children some pictures of different rivers and discuss them.
● Look together at the illustration of the family crossing the river in the story. Why have the characters taken off their shoes? How will they feel when they get out of the water? Why is it dangerous crossing a river like that?
● Ask the children if they can remember the two words that are used to describe the river. ('Deep' and 'cold'.) Encourage the children to think of other words that could be used, for example 'fast' and 'wide' and write them on the flipchart.
● Remind the children of the words used to describe the sound made by the family going through the river: 'Splash, splosh!'. Why do they think the author chose these words? What could be used instead?
● Give out the photocopiable sheet and ask the children to complete it, using their own ideas.
● Ask some children to share their 'deep', 'cold' and 'splash splosh!' words, then to read their new sentences. Why did they choose those words?

Differentiation
For older/more able children: Discuss the idea of adjectives and ask the children to begin a collection of similar words.
For younger/less able children: Let the children role-play the journey through the river.

What are they thinking?

Objective: To consider how settings influence events and behaviour.
What you need: Photocopiable page 18, writing materials, flipchart, prepared large, blank thought bubble, copies of *We're Going on a Bear Hunt*.
Cross-curricular links: Science, Unit 1D, Light and dark, Citizenship, Unit 02, Choices.

What to do

● Hold up the thought bubble and ask what it is. How is it different from a speech bubble in appearance? Where are speech and thought bubbles usually found? (In comics.)
● Put the thought bubble above your head and ask the children to suggest what you might be thinking. Write in one of their suggestions.
● Turn to the double-page spread in the story that has the text: 'Uh-uh! Mud!'. Draw the children's attention to the father and ask for ideas as to what he might be thinking. Draw a thought bubble on the flipchart and write one of the suggestions in it.
● Give out the photocopiable sheet and explain to the children that you want them to write in the thought bubbles what the characters might be thinking. Point out that only four characters have thought bubbles. Ensure children understand that the smaller bubbles join the person with their thoughts. It may be necessary to have a short discussion about the cave and how the characters might be feeling apprehensive as they go in it.
● Discuss the children's varying ideas as a class.

Differentiation
For older/more able children: Ask the children to write a description of the inside of a cave.
For younger/less able children: Let the children work with a partner to complete the photocopiable sheet.

Plot, character and setting

Write a blurb

Objectives: To compare books, to evaluate, giving reasons; to use 'blurbs'.
What you need: Books with good back-cover blurbs, copies of *We're Going on a Bear Hunt*, individual whiteboards, writing materials.
Cross-curricular links: Art and design.

What to do

● Ask the children what the writing on the back of a book is for. (It describes some of the events in the story.) Explain that this writing is called a blurb.
● Show the front cover of one of your selected books. Read the title to the children and ask what they think the story could be about. Illustrations can also provide an indication. Turn the book over and read out the blurb. Were the children right? Repeat with other books.
● Discuss with the children why the blurb is important. (The reader can easily find out what the story is about and decide if they would like to read it.)
● Point out that sometimes blurbs include quotes from other sources about the book. On a whiteboard ask the children to write their own quote for *We're Going on a Bear Hunt*.
● Look together at the back of *We're Going on a Bear Hunt*. Say that it does not tell the reader very much about the story. Invite the children to make suggestions for a new blurb, describing some of the events and characters. Ask the children to compose their own blurb, including their quote.
● Share the children's different blurbs. Do they give different impressions of the book?

Differentiation
For older/more able children: Ask the children to include two quotes from other children in the class.
For younger/less able children: Let the children design a new front cover for the book.

The zigzag book

Objective: To understand time and sequential relationships in stories.
What you need: Flipchart, word cards for: 'First', 'Then', 'Next', 'After that', 'Finally', copies of *We're Going on a Bear Hunt*, prepared blank zigzag books, writing and drawing materials.
Cross-curricular links: Art and design.

What to do

● Ask the children to think of five things they have done that day in the order they have done them. Invite a volunteer to write their list on the flipchart.
● Show the children your word cards. Discuss how these words describe the passage of time. Ask the children to put the words in the correct sequence in front of the lists of events.
● Look at *We're Going on a Bear Hunt* together and identify the places the family go through. Write them on the flipchart in the correct order. Display the word cards ask the children to think about which event would match each card.
● Show the children how to make a book (by folding a piece of paper four times concertina-style). Hand out the prepared blank zigzag books and writing and drawing materials. Ask the children to make a simple version of the story by writing a sentence and drawing a picture, of some of the events in the correct order.
● Look at the different books and share some of them as a class. Display the books to remind children of the story and its sequence.

Differentiation
For older/more able children: Encourage the children to use four out of the five words or phrases on the word cards.
For younger/less able children: Make a group zigzag book.

Plot, character and setting

I like this book because…

> **Objective:** To express their views about a story.
> **What you need:** Whiteboards and pens, flipchart, writing materials.
> **Cross-curricular links:** Citizenship, Unit 02, Choices; PSHE.

What to do

● Ask the children for personal opinions on their enjoyment of the story. On their individual whiteboard, ask them to write down their favourite part.
● Encourage the children to share their thoughts with the rest of the class. Did everybody pick the same bit? Why not?
● Write on the flipchart the headings: 'Characters', 'Plot' and 'Setting'. Do the children know what each of the headings mean?
● Invite the children to give you examples from the book to go under each heading.

(For example: Characters: bear, children; Plot: looking for a bear, finding it and it chasing the family; Setting: river, forest.)
● Ask if there was any part of the story the children did not like. Why did they not like it? Discuss the characters and ask the children to comment on anything they disliked about them. Continue to do the same with plot and setting.
● Can the children give an evaluation of the book based on what they have discussed? (For example: 'I like this book because the bear chases the family.') Share these evaluations and ask the children to write their sentences down.

> **Differentiation**
> **For older/more able children:** Ask the children to write some sentences about the book using the words 'character', 'plot' and 'setting'.
> **For younger/less able children:** Provide a framework for the children to complete simple sentences about the book.

Illustrations

> **Objective:** To use story settings from reading, for example, use in own writing.
> **What you need:** Writing materials, whiteboards and pens, copies of *We're Going on a Bear Hunt*.
> **Cross-curricular links:** Art and design.

What to do

● Read the story to the children without showing them the illustrations. Ask whether they enjoyed the story as much as when they heard it read aloud the first time and were allowed to see the illustrations.
● Re-read the book, showing the pictures. If possible use a Big Book version. Encourage the children to discuss the illustrations, and to comment on how the pictures contribute to their understanding of the story. For example: the happy faces as they run through the grass; the worried looks in the snowstorm; the bear's face as he looks at the dog.

● Choose an illustration and ask the children to suggest details that could be added to the text, based on the picture. Suggestions could be written on whiteboards and recorded on a flipchart. Do you think that the illustration is as important if you have the details in the text?
● Select another illustration and display it where all the children can see it. Ask them to write some extra text to support the illustration. Remind them to look at the whole illustration.
● Share the children's sentences. Discuss the different effects their sentences create. Do they think that the words or the illustrations are more effective?

> **Differentiation**
> **For older/more able children:** Ask the children to include some speech in their writing.
> **For younger/less able children:** Working with an adult, let the children complete simple sentences in a shared-writing activity.

Plot, character and setting

What now?

Draw and label two other places the family could have gone through on their bear hunt.

Write the rhyme for one of your choices, choosing two words to describe it.

Uh-uh! A _____

A _____ _____ _____

We can't go _____

We can't go _____

Oh no! _____

It's a bear!

Think of some words that could be used to describe the bear in the cave.

big

brown

Illustration © Helen Oxenbury

Describe the bear using some of the words from above.

_____

_____

_____

_____

The river

Uh-uh! A river!
A deep cold river.

Splash splosh!
Splash splosh!
Splash splosh!

Text © Michael Rosen

In the box on the right write some words that could be used to describe the river instead of **deep** and **cold**.

Think of some other words that could be used instead of **Splash splosh!** that would describe the noise made by the family as they go through the river.

Choose new words to replace **deep** and **cold** and **Splash splosh!** from the boxes above and write out your new rhyme about the river on a separate piece of paper. Illustrate your rhyme.

What are they thinking?

Write in the thought bubbles what the characters might be thinking as they go into the gloomy cave.

Illustration © Helen Oxenbury

READ & RESPOND: Activities based on We're Going on a Bear Hunt

Talk about it

What are they saying?

> **Objectives:** To retell stories; to identify and discuss characters.
> **What you need:** Photocopiable page 22, copies of *We're Going on a Bear Hunt*, flipchart and pen.
> **Cross-curricular links:** Drama; PSHE.

What to do
● Look together at the double-page spread in the story where the family arrives back at the house and run up the stairs. Discuss what is happening in the pictures.
● Say you are going to talk together about how the children might be feeling being chased by a bear. Are they scared? Will they feel safe now they have reached their own home? Look at the first illustration and discuss what the two children at the bottom of the stairs might be saying. (For example: 'Run quickly!' 'Oh no! We forgot to shut the door!')
● Ask how they could show what the characters are saying on the illustration. (Speech bubbles.)

Draw two large speech bubbles on the flipchart. Invite the children to offer suggestions as to what you could write in them. Choose two and write one in each of the speech bubbles.
● Give out the photocopiable sheet and explain that the children need to think about what the characters might be saying.
● Ask the children to work with a talk partner to discuss their ideas before completing their sheet. Encourage them to write different ideas from their partners.
● Discuss the children's different ideas. What do the children think they would say in that situation?

> **Differentiation**
> **For older/more able children:** Ask the children to discuss what happens to the bear after he is locked out of the house.
> **For younger/less able children:** Invite the children role-play the scene with an adult playing the part of the father.

The puzzle

> **Objective:** To discuss meanings of words and phrases, and sound effects in poetry.
> **What you need:** Photocopiable page 23, copies of *We're Going on a Bear Hunt*, flipchart and pen.
> **Cross-curricular links:** Drama.

What to do
● Read the story with the children joining in with the rhyme.
● Write on a flipchart the words: 'grass', 'river', 'mud' 'forest' and 'snowstorm'. Ask the children to recall the sounds that are linked to these places. ('Swishy swashy!' and so on.)
● Working with a talk partner, ask the children to discuss different actions that could be used to enhance the above words (for example, 'Splash splosh!' could shown by stamping feet). Ask the pairs to agree on one action to perform together,

with one child saying the words and the other performing the actions. Invite volunteers to show the class.
● Hand out the photocopiable sheet. Encourage the children to work in their pairs to fill in the missing words and cut out and complete the puzzle.
● Ask the children if they think the story is better with actions. Which actions do they think are best? Re-read the story together with the children performing their actions.

> **Differentiation**
> **For older/more able children:** Ask the children, in pairs, to mime the journey through the various places for others to guess.
> **For younger/less able children:** Let the children work with an adult to complete the photocopiable sheet.

Talk about it

Putting on a play

> **Objective:** To prepare and retell stories through role-play in groups.
> **What you need:** Photocopiable page 24, copies of *We're Going on a Bear Hunt*, flipchart and pen, musical instruments, props.
> **Cross-curricular links:** Drama; Music, Unit 2, Sounds interesting – Exploring sounds.

What to do

● Read through *We're Going on a Bear Hunt*. Make a list together of all the characters that appear in the story.
● Choose one character and, using one of the illustrations from the book, ask the children to describe what the character is doing. Repeat with other characters.
● Explain that the children are going to act out the story in small groups. Ask if they have ever seen a play performed. What is meant by the word 'cast'? Do they know what a director is?

● Say that each group should select a director, who will be in charge of choosing the roles for the rest of the group but will not take part in the performance.
● Encourage the children to consider props and musical instruments that may support their performance.
● Allow the children to go off into their groups and complete the photocopiable sheet together and then rehearse their play.
● Each group can perform their play to the rest of the class.

> **Differentiation**
> **For older/more able children:** Ask children to become 'theatre critics' and talk about the performances of other groups. Ensure the children understand that they should make positive comments.
> **For younger/less able children:** Let the children work as a group with an adult as the director.

The broadcast

> **Objectives:** To notice the difference between spoken and written forms through retelling; to discuss patterns of rhythm and other features.
> **What you need:** Copies of *We're Going on a Bear Hunt*, tape recorder with microphone, musical instruments.
> **Cross-curricular links:** Drama; Music, Unit 2, Sounds interesting – Exploring sounds.

What to do

● Choose together one of the places the family go through (for example, the river). Practise saying the rhyme as a class and then explain that you are going to record the children saying the rhyme.
● Record their performance and then play it back for the children to listen to and discuss. Ask for suggestions and for improvements. Re-record the verse.

● Show the children a selection of musical instruments and ask how these could be used to enhance the performance.
● Explain to the children that they are going to work in groups, each taking a different part of the story to record. Give the children some rehearsal time before recording their performance.
● Bring the children back together and listen to each group's broadcast in turn. Discuss, as a class, encouraging positive comments.

> **Differentiation**
> **For older/more able children:** Make a 'radio broadcast' of the performance with a presenter making an introduction, the children performing the full text, and interviews afterwards with children explaining their different roles.
> **For younger/less able children:** Ask an adult to say the text, with the children playing musical instruments at appropriate moments.

Talk about it

Interview with the bear

> **Objective:** To prepare and retell stories through role-play in groups.
> **What you need:** Whiteboards and pens, copies of *We're Going on a Bear Hunt*.
> **Cross-curricular links:** Drama; PSHE.

What to do
● Read the end of the story from where the bear appears.
● Encourage the children to focus on this part of the story. Look through the final few illustrations. As a class, discuss what happens and how the bear responds to the situation.
● Ask the children to work with a talk partner to consider the bear's thoughts and feelings. Then to share these ideas as a class.
● Give each child a whiteboard and pen and encourage them to write a question they would like to ask the bear. (For example: 'How did you feel when you saw the people at the cave?' 'Why did you chase after the family?')
● Organise the children into small groups and ask them to take it in turns to be the bear answering the other children's prepared questions.
● Circulate among the groups, making sure all the children take part in the role-play.
● Discuss the activity as a class. Do the children think that this brought the bear to life? How did it feel to be the bear? Have their opinions of the bear changed?

> **Differentiation**
> **For older/more able children:** Repeat the activity, role-playing one of the other characters in the story.
> **For younger/less able children:** Ask an adult to play the part of the bear.

A crocodile hunt!

> **Objective:** To retell stories orally, identifying and using some of the features of story language.
> **What you need:** Whiteboards and pens.
> **Cross-curricular links:** Drama.

What to do
● Ask the children to consider what might happen the day after the bear hunt, when one of the children went to school and told the events of the previous day. How do they think the other children listening would respond? Would they believe the story?
● Put the children into small groups. Explain to the children that they are going to tell a short story orally, based on *We're Going on a Bear Hunt*. This story will be called: We're going on a crocodile hunt!
● Discuss, as a class, some ideas about 'We're going on a crocodile hunt'. Where could a crocodile live? Who will your characters be? What sorts of things might the characters have to travel through?
● Ask the children to discuss and agree in their groups what happens in their story and how they are going to retell it. Say that they can make notes on their whiteboards and that all the children should take part. Try to encourage the children to think of their own ideas rather than just taking ideas straight from the board.
● Allow time for the children to rehearse their ideas.
● Let each group perform their version to the rest of the class.
● Ask those listening to be a 'good audience'. Encourage the children to ask and answer questions at the end of each story retelling. Such as: Why did you decide the crocodile was going to live in a swamp?

> **Differentiation**
> **For older/more able children:** Ask the children to tell their story as if it happened the day before and they are retelling it to their friends at school.
> **For younger/less able children:** Let the children work with an adult to support them in their retelling.

What are they saying?

Write in the speech bubbles what the characters might be saying as they try to shut the door.

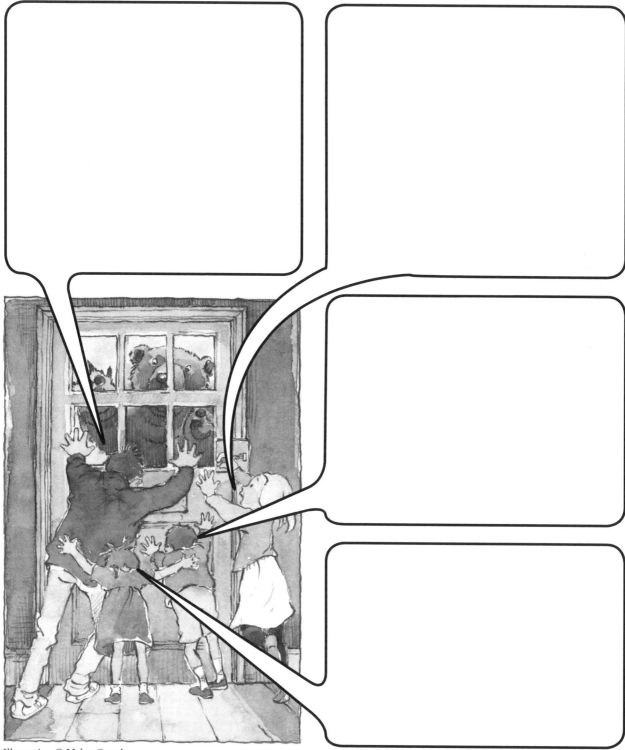

Illustration © Helen Oxenbury

READ & RESPOND: Activities based on We're Going on a Bear Hunt

SECTION
5

The puzzle

Complete the phrases. Cut them out and match them to the correct sound effect.

A deep	Splash splosh!
A big	Swishy swashy!
The long	Hoooo woooo!
A gloomy	Squelch squerch!
A swirling	Tiptoe tiptoe!
The thick	Stumble trip!

Putting on a play

Director

Cast

Dad _____

Girl 1 _____

Girl 2 _____

Boy _____

Baby _____

Bear _____

Dog (optional) _____

Props needed	Musical instruments

Get writing

What happened next?

Objective: To use story settings from reading to use in own writing.
What you need: Photocopiable page 28, writing and drawing materials, whiteboards and pens, copies of *We're Going on a Bear Hunt*.
Cross-curricular links: Citizenship, Unit 02, Choices; PSHE.

What to do

● Look together at the illustration of the family back at home with the bear coming towards the open door. Ask the question: 'What is going to happen next?'
● Discuss with the children why the bear might have followed the family to their home. How might the bear be feeling? (Angry for being disturbed? Lonely and looking for friends?)
● Ask the children to work in pairs, using a whiteboard, to list words to describe how the bear might be feeling as he comes towards the door and the family rush to close it. (For example: sad, lonely, miserable, mad, furious, wild.) Point out that the bear could be feeling lots of different emotions at the same time.
● Explain that how the bear feels will influence what he does next. Ask the children to suggest what might happen after the bear has gotten to the door.
● Hand out the photocopiable sheet and ask the children to work on their own, writing down what happened next.

Differentiation
For older/more able children: Ask the children to choose one of the things they described and to develop it further.
For younger/less able children: Let the children draw a picture to illustrate one of their descriptions.

The same and different

Objective: To write non-fiction texts.
What you need: Photocopiable page 29, non-fiction books about animals, writing materials, flipchart and pen.
Cross-curricular links: Science, Unit 2C, Variation.

What to do

● Discuss with the children what category of books *We're Going on a Bear Hunt* would fall into. (Fiction.) Ask them to explain what makes it a fiction book.
● Display your non-fiction books and ask the children to describe what type of books these are, and how they differ from *We're Going on a Bear Hunt*.
● Look at the illustration of the bear as it comes out of the cave in *We're Going on a Bear Hunt*. Ask the children to describe the bear and to give you any other information they know about bears in general.
● Write the headings 'Same' and 'Different' on a flipchart. Discuss the meaning of these two words. Choose an animal such as an elephant as an example and discuss the similarities and differences between the children and the elephant. (For example, 'We both have skin.') Record the statements under the correct headings on the flipchart. If necessary, repeat with other animals.
● Hand out the photocopiable sheet and explain to the children that you want them to do the same for a bear.
● Discuss the children's ideas about what is the same or different between them and a bear. Are lots of things the same, or are most different?

Differentiation
For older/more able children: Ask the children to write a piece of non-fiction about bears.
For younger/less able children: Modify the activity as a piece of shared writing with an adult.

Get writing

We're going on a...hunt

> **Objective:** To use story settings from reading to write a different story.
> **What you need:** Photocopiable page 30, writing materials, flipchart and pen.
> **Cross-curricular links:** Geography, Unit 7, Weather around the world; Unit 24, Passport to the world.

What to do
- Discuss with the children the settings used in the story. Ask them to describe the features of each place (for example, *long* grass).
- Invite the children to suggest different problems in different settings that the characters might have to overcome (for example: a jungle, a thunderstorm, a desert). On a flipchart make a collection of descriptive words.
- The family were going on a bear hunt. Discuss with the children other animals they could hunt for, encouraging them to select animals that are scary, fierce or funny.

- Encourage the children to recall the repetitive phrase that begins: 'We're going on a bear hunt…'. Choose one of the following words: 'big', 'beautiful' or 'scared'. Ask the children to suggest alternative words.
- Explain to the children that, using *We're Going on a Bear Hunt* as a model, they are going to make some notes on the photocopiable sheet to plan a new story.
- Point out that they need to choose three settings and an animal before writing the repeated phrase and story ending.
- Discuss the different animals the children chose and the places the journey took them.

> **Differentiation**
> **For older/more able children:** Challenge the children to use the completed plan to write their own story.
> **For younger/less able children:** Provide adult support for writing. Let the children plan their story by drawing pictures to represent each scene.

The snowstorm

> **Objective:** To use structures from poems as a basis for writing.
> **What you need:** Writing materials, flipchart, whiteboards and pens, copies of *We're Going on a Bear Hunt*.
> **Cross-curricular links:** Geography, Unit 7, Weather around the world.

What to do
- Look together at the two pages showing the snowstorm. Ask who has seen snow and who hasn't. Has anyone ever been caught in a real snowstorm? What was it like?
- Ask how the children would they feel if they were caught in a snowstorm. Encourage them to find the two words that describe the snowstorm. ('Swirling' and 'whirling'.) What do the words 'Hoooo wooooo!' mean?
- Ask the children to work in pairs to list on

a whiteboard other words that could describe a snowstorm. Encourage the children to choose words that end in '-*ing*'.
- Listen to the children's ideas and record them on a flipchart.
- Give the children writing materials and explain that you want them to write some short sentences or a poem to describe a snowstorm. They should use some of the words collected together. An example could be:
Twisting, twirling snowstorm
Howling, blowing snowstorm
Freezing, perishing snowstorm
Weaving, curling snowstorm.

> **Differentiation**
> **For older/more able children:** Challenge the children to write in a similar way about one of the other settings.
> **For younger/less able children:** Work together to produce a group piece of writing.

Get writing

Chased by a bear

> **Objectives:** To use the past tense consistently; to secure the use of sentences in their own writing.
> **What you need:** Writing materials, flipchart, whiteboards and pens, simple newspaper reports.
> **Cross-curricular links:** Citizenship, Unit 11, In the media – what's the news?; Geography, Unit 16, What's the news?

What to do
● Ask the children if they get a newspaper at home. List some of the things that are written about in newspapers (for example: accidents, sports events and disasters).
● Look together at the newspaper reports collected. Point out the main features of a newspaper report: headline, subheading, columns of writing and pictures.
● Ask the children what the people who write in newspapers are called. (Reporters.) Read through one of the articles and look for quotes from people being interviewed, descriptions of surroundings and what news is being reported.
● Explain to the children that they are going to pretend to be a newspaper reporter and write a report based on an interview with one of the family from *We're Going on a Bear Hunt.*
● Let the children work in pairs to plan a headline for the report, using their whiteboards. Ask volunteers to share their ideas with the class.
● Hand out writing materials and ask the children to write a short report. Encourage the children to plan their piece first.

> **Differentiation**
> **For older/more able children:** Ask the children to continue the report by interviewing the bear.
> **For younger/less able children:** As a group, write some captions for possible photographs.

The letter

> **Objective:** To use story settings from reading to use in own writing.
> **What you need:** Writing materials, flipchart, copies of *We're Going on a Bear Hunt.*
> **Cross-curricular links:** Citizenship, Unit 02, Choices; PSHE; ICT, Unit 2A, Communicating information using text – word process letter to bear.

What to do
● Look together at the end of the story, as the family rush home and lock the bear out. Discuss with the children how the characters are feeling. (Relieved, happy to be home, safe.)
● Ask the children to consider what might happen the next day. The family might start to think about the feelings of the bear. Perhaps the bear wasn't as fierce as they first thought, maybe he wanted to be friends. Perhaps the bear was scared of them? Had they upset the bear?
● Explain to the children that they are going to write a letter to the bear from the family. Discuss what they might include in the letter: an explanation of what they had been doing that day; that they did not mean to scare the bear; that they hoped they had not hurt the bear's feelings. How are they going to make things better? They could invite the bear round for tea!
● Model the beginning of a letter on the flipchart. Then hand out writing materials and ask the children to complete the letter on their own.
● Ask the children to share their letters. Discuss the different ideas for making amends.

> **Differentiation**
> **For older/more able children:** Ask the children to write a reply from the bear.
> **For younger/less able children:** Write a simple invitation for the bear to come to tea.

What happened next?

Look at the picture of the bear about to come through the door. Write about four different things that could happen next.

1.

2.

3.

4.

Illustration © Helen Oxenbury

SCHOLASTIC
www.scholastic.co.uk

SECTION
6

The same and different

Some things about you and a bear are the same. Some things are different. Write three more things in the boxes below.

I have two eyes.	A bear has two eyes.
I go to school.	A bear does not go to school.
•	•
•	•
•	•

Get writing

We're going on a...hunt

Plan your own story based on *We're Going on a Bear Hunt.* Draw the animal the characters are going to hunt.

Write three different places the characters go through.

Choose some different words to put in the repeated phrase.

We're going on a _____ hunt.

We're going to catch a _____ one.

What a _____ day!

We're not _____ .

Describe how your story ends.

_____

_____

_____

Assessment

Assessment advice

Assessing a child's progress is a necessary part of school life for children and teachers alike. There are two types of assessment: formal (SATs) and teacher assessments, both ongoing.

The purpose of assessment is to inform the teacher of the level of progress a child is making and influence future planning for that child. Outcomes of assessments can enable teachers to set new targets for each child. Teachers need to ensure that children are progressing and receiving the best and most appropriate level of support. It is also important for children to be involved in their own assessments and to be encouraged by their learning.

Reporting and teacher assessment need to be based on evidence, which should be drawn from a child's practical work and from classroom discussion.

In *Read & Respond* the children are offered a variety of activities to further develop speaking and listening, and reading and writing skills. These areas can all be assessed using written assessments, and classroom observations of group, paired and individual activities. The assessment activity on photocopiable page 32 could be used as part of a record of individual children's progress. By using this approach, you can integrate purposeful application of knowledge and skills, differentiation, assessment and record keeping.

What do you remember?

> **Objectives:** To show understanding of story elements; to write in sentences using capital letters and full stops accurately.
> **Resources:** Photocopiable page 32, writing materials.

What to do

● As part of an assessment of the work the children have completed on *We're Going on a Bear Hunt*, discuss the various features and events within the story. It will be possible to make some judgements based on the children's verbal responses.

● Ask for personal opinions on their enjoyment of the story (do not focus too much on any particular aspects of the story as this may influence their performance in the written assessment).

● Discuss the different things an author needs to think about when writing a story. Encourage the children to talk about characters, events and settings. Make sure they understand that this can apply to any type of story they may have read.

● Choose a book the children have recently read together. Ask them to give the name of the author, illustrator and who published the book and take some time to discuss the roles of each.

● Discuss in general the features of the story *We're Going on a Bear Hunt*. This could include characters, setting and events. Ask the children questions about the story but make sure you do not refer to the specific questions on the photocopiable sheet.

● Before giving out photocopiable page 32, remind the children about answering the questions in complete sentences. Stress the fact that you do not want to see one-word answers.

SECTION 7

What do you remember?

Answer each of the following questions about *We're Going on a Bear Hunt*. Remember to use complete sentences.

Who is the <u>author</u> of *We're Going on a Bear Hunt*?

_____

Who is the <u>illustrator</u> of *We're Going on a Bear Hunt*?

_____

Who <u>published</u> *We're Going on a Bear Hunt*?

_____

How many people went on the bear hunt?

_____

What did the children take off to go through the river?

_____

What did they forget to do when they ran upstairs?

_____

What colour was the dog in the story?

_____